GUNK ALIENS

THE ELEPHANT'S TRUMP

Collect all the books in the *GUNK Aliens* series!

JONNY MOON

GUNK ALIENS

THE ELEPHANT'S TRUMP

HarperCollins *Children's Books*

First published in paperback in Great Britain by
HarperCollins *Children's Books* 2009
HarperCollins *Children's Books* is a division of HarperCollins*Publishers* Ltd
77-85 Fulham Palace Road, Hammersmith, London W6 8JB

The HarperCollins website address is:

www.harpercollins.co.uk

1

Copyright © HarperCollins 2009
Illustrations by Vincent Vigla
Illustrations © HarperCollins 2009

ISBN: 978-0-00-731095-1

Printed and bound in England by Clays Ltd, St Ives plc

Special thanks to Colin Brake,
GUNGE agent extraordinaire.

A long time ago, in a galaxy far, far away, a bunch of slimy aliens discovered the secret to clean, renewable energy...

... snot!

(Well, OK, clean-*ish*.)

There was just one problem. The best snot came from only one kind of creature.

Humans.

And humans were very rare. Within a few years, the aliens had used up all the best snot in their solar system.

That was when the Galactic Union of Nasty Killer Aliens (GUNK) was born. Its mission: to find human life and drain its snot. Rockets were sent to the four corners of the universe, each carrying representatives from the major alien races. Three of those rockets were never heard from again. But one of them landed on a planet quite simply *full* of humans.

This one.

CHAPTER ONE

It started like any other Saturday, but for Jack Brady this particular weekend was the beginning of an adventure he would never forget.

Jack Brady didn't *look* particularly special, but he was.

Jack was nine years old, slightly less than average height for his age and had the usual

number of facial features in the usual sort of arrangement. His friend Ruby said he had 'very striking blue eyes', but the optician had just called them lazy and so he wore glasses most of the time. This gave Jack a slightly geeky look, but he didn't mind too much because he was, in his spare time, a genius.

Jack was an inventor, always busy creating new ideas and improving old ones. It was this – his inventing – that he was sure would, in time, be the making of him. But for now he had an even more important role to perform. He was an agent of GUNGE – a dedicated but secret organisation that was engaged in vital work to protect Planet Earth from alien attack.

Jack had only recently been recruited into the fight – a struggle he had thought a joke at first. Until, that was, he'd met an alien face to face. Helped by his best friend Oscar and his new friend Ruby, Jack had defeated the deadly Squillibloat – a terrifying and frankly gross cross between an octopus and a jellyfish – and saved the day. Since then he had been on a constant state of alert, waiting for his next mission from the mysterious Bob, his contact at GUNGE.

But that had been nearly a week ago. Since then everything had been quiet. Only the presence of his new pet – Snivel – reminded him that the whole thing had been real and not a terrible dream. Snivel was a transforming robot created by GUNGE from alien technology. In his dog form, he helped Jack by giving useful information about the aliens he was supposed to capture. But he also helped out with the capturing bit – in a very direct way! When Jack spoke the words 'Activate Snivel Trap', Snivel could instantly transform from a dog into an alien trap, ready to suck up any hostile alien.

The only problem was that Snivel had to be directly underneath the alien when activated – something that had made catching the Squillibloat in the local swimming pool a bit of a task. Jack hadn't thought his invention of a canine scuba suit would *ever* come in useful...

Actually, that wasn't the only problem. The even bigger problem was that a mistake by GUNGE had caused Snivel to be built with three eyes in his dog form.

CLUNK!

For the forty-second time in the last hour Snivel fell sideways to the floor. He was trying to keep his third eye closed – Jack had told him it would help him blend in – but try as he might he couldn't seem to manage it without losing his balance.

"Give it a rest, Snivel," Jack said.

"I thought it was important?" replied the robot dog.

"It is, but if you keep banging the floor like that Mum's going to go mad."

TAP! TAP!

"*Now* what are you doing?" asked Jack.

"Me?" said Snivel in an offended tone. "Nothing."

TAP! TAP! TAP!

"Is that your tail banging the floor?"

"No!"

TAP! TAP! TAP!

"Are you sure?"

Snivel span around, trying to catch sight of his tail. "I think so…"

TAP! TAP! TAP!

Jack held his finger up to his lips. "Ssh!" he said.

TAP! TAP! TAP!

The noise was coming from the window. Jack crossed the room and yanked it open.

"Oscar, go away," he began but the figure climbing into the room was not that of his best friend. The legs were dressed in pink leg-warmers and the rest of the outfit included a leopard-print skirt. It was Ruby! She seemed to be dressed for some kind of dance lesson, except for two key elements of her appearance.

"Check this out," she said enthusiastically, showing him her feet and her hands. The latter were chalky white and when she clapped them together a little cloud of dust rose into the air. Her shoes were some kind of specialist trainer, with a unique gripping sole. Both the shoes and the chalky hands were totally out of sync with the rest of the outfit.

Jack shrugged. "You've been working out in a circus?" he wondered.

Ruby shook her head. "No, silly. These are climber's shoes."

"You've been to climbing lessons in *that* gear?" He looked at her leopard-print skirt. It clashed quite badly with the pink leg-warmers – even Jack could see that, and he was a boy.

"Mum thinks I'm doing something called modern jazz dance," explained Ruby.

That made more sense. Jack hadn't known Ruby that long but one thing he did know about the pretty dark-skinned girl was that she loved dangerous sports but her mum would never let her do anything but  safe, girly activities. So Ruby maintained a complicated scheme of little white lies: her ballet classes were really a cover for surfing lessons, and now "modern jazz dance" was obviously a disguise for...

"Climbing lessons. I've only been going for a couple of weeks."

"And you just climbed up here?" Jack asked. Ruby nodded proudly.

"But this is two floors up!" said Jack.

"Yeah…" Ruby shrugged and grinned. "But you have to start small, don't you?"

Jack rolled his eyes and then a thought occurred to him.

"Isn't it unsafe to climb alone? Shouldn't you have a partner with you?"

"I do…" Ruby began but she was unable to finish her sentence as there was a loud crash from outside.

Jack rushed over to the window and looked out. Sprawled on the bins below his window was Oscar. He waved a cheery hand.

Ruby joined Jack at the window. "He has a way to go," she conceded.

"Yes," said Jack. "Up the stairs, it looks like."

Oscar started to get to his feet.

"I'll get the hang of it in a minute," he insisted.

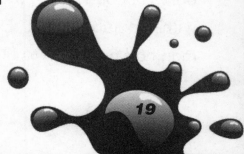

19

Jack shook his head. "Wait there," he told his friend. "Snivel needs a walk, we'll come down to you."

Ruby began to climb out of the window. Jack grabbed her arm. "Not that way!"

A few moments later the three of them, along with Snivel, were heading for the park. They didn't need to discuss where they were going, as each of them knew exactly where they wanted to go – and why. They were hoping to meet Bob – the mysterious GUNGE agent who would have the details of the next mission for them.

Once inside the park they headed for the area where they had last had contact with Bob. Previously Bob had talked to them from within a rubbish bin. Exactly how a grown man had managed to fit inside a park rubbish bin they had never asked.

But now it looked as if it was too late to ask any such questions. The bin – Bob's bin – was no longer there. Bob had disappeared!

CHAPTER TWO

The three children stood in stunned silence around the space where Bob's bin had been. Finally Oscar spoke.

"It's gone!"

"Yeah, we noticed, Einstein!" said Ruby a little unkindly.

"But how are we going to find out about out next mission now?" Oscar continued, oblivious to Ruby's comment.

Jack bit his lip. Bob had promised that he'd be in touch – and soon. Although they had successfully captured the Squillibloat and retrieved its segment of the Blower, the intergalactic phone that would summon a full scale invasion, there were still three different aliens, with three different bits of the Blower still at large.

"I guess it's not so urgent now," Ruby decided. "I mean, Bob's got the first bit of the Blower safely locked away so the others can't put their bits together and make it work, can they?"

"I don't know," answered Jack honestly. "Snivel?"

Snivel scratched his head with a back paw. "If the aliens get together with the other bits of the Blower they might be able to rig up a makeshift component to make it work. They may well be very stupid, and they definitely hate each other, but if they thought they could get hold of all the snot you humans make they might just find a way."

Snot was what the aliens were all about. It was the key to their technology, the energy source they needed to power everything. There were four alien races in the alliance known as GUNK. Together they were the Galactic Union of Nasty Killer Aliens and they were on a mission – to seek out snot! If GUNK were able to mount a full-scale invasion of Earth, then pretty soon every single human being on the planet would be hooked up to a revolting milking machine, to suck the snot out of their heads.

Unluckily, a GUNK scout ship had recently discovered Earth – and had landed right on Jack's town!

Luckily, it hadn't really *landed* so much as *crashed*. The four aliens on board had been scattered by the explosion. And, because they didn't trust each other, they each had one part of the Blower – the device that would allow them to tell their friends back home that they'd found a whole planet full of snot. Bob had explained to Jack and his friends that, as agents of GUNGE (the General Under-Committee for the Neutralisation of Gruesome Extraterrestrials), they needed to find the aliens, trap them using Snivel and capture the components of the Blower before they could be united to send that message back to their home planets.

But now Bob was gone.

Snivel's third eye snapped wide open and began to glow red.

Jack bent down to take a closer look.

"Are you all right?" he asked.

But something peculiar was happening to Snivel. He seemed

entranced and his gaze was fixed on some point across the path, behind them. Jack turned around to see what it was that his robot dog was looking at. At first he couldn't see anything but then he looked down. There – standing on the grass – was a squirrel. There was something very odd about this particular squirrel. For one thing it was not afraid of the humans. And beyond that, it was looking, *really* looking, at each of them in turn. As Jack watched, the squirrel turned its gaze first on Ruby, then Oscar and finally himself before looking back towards Snivel. And now the squirrel seemed to be making some kind of gesture with his little paws, almost as if he was… *beckoning?*

Suddenly the squirrel took off, running away at speed and before Jack could say or do anything Snivel sped off in pursuit. Jack, taken by surprise, was jerked along by the lead and,

like an anchor being pulled behind a ship, he collided with his friends, knocking them all to the ground. He lost his grip on the handle of his dog lead and could only watch as Snivel disappeared around a hedge.

Quickly, the three children got to their feet and set off to follow the squirrel-chasing robot dog. The chase took them in and out of the hedge maze, through the ornamental garden and around the boating lake. At one point they nearly ran into the park keeper, but when he saw that the children running towards him included Jack and Oscar, the uniformed man turned tail and hid in his equipment shed.

Finally the trail led out of the park completely. Jack was beginning to run out of breath. Oscar ran ahead and called back, "He's heading for the canal!"

Ruby had stopped to make sure Jack was all right. "Come on," she said encouragingly, "he can't get too far." Jack instantly realised that she was right. The canal disappeared into an industrial park a few hundred metres from the park, and the public access towpath terminated in a dead end. Gathering himself for one last effort he started jogging again. Oscar was already on the towpath when he got there.

"Where... where'd he go?" gasped Jack, feeling very unfit and not at all like a top agent of GUNGE. First he'd lost his contact and now it looked like he was going to lose his robot dog. Things were not going well.

Oscar shrugged, and looked embarrassed.

"I don't know," he confessed. "He went that way..." Oscar pointed off towards the dead end of the towpath. "... but now I can't see him!"

Ruby joined them. "What about up there?" She was looking towards a footbridge which led over the canal and into a housing estate. "He must have gone that way."

She led the way up the metal steps and across the bridge and on the other side they found themselves in a narrow alley. The alley twisted and turned and eventually they exited into a street of modern houses. And there, sitting beneath a red pillar box, was Snivel.

His exhaustion forgotten in his relief, Jack ran up to Snivel and gave him a hug.

"At last," boomed a familiar voice. "I was beginning to think you'd never get here."

The voice was coming from the postbox. And it belonged to Bob! After greeting the three young agents, Bob explained that for security reasons he had to move his base of operations around.

"Are you really inside there?" asked Ruby. She hadn't spoken to Bob last time around – she'd only ended up joining Jack and Oscar because she followed them at the pool, and helped them to catch the Squillibloat.

"Of course I am," replied Bob, "and I keep getting letters landing on my head to prove it. But it's an improvement on being hidden in a rubbish bin, I can tell you."

showered with empty crisp packets and cans of pop all the time in his last base.

"What was wrong with Snivel just then?" asked Jack, remembering the strange look that had been in the robot dog's eyes back in the park. "He saw this weird squirrel thing and then he went running off."

"Nothing's wrong with him," Bob told them, "he's just been downloaded with all the necessary data for your next mission."

"You've got another alien for us to find?" asked Oscar keenly.

"Yes," said Bob. "Your next target has been identified. And you must remember to get hold of the Blower segment that the alien is carrying. The three remaining bits can still be made to work together if the aliens manage to meet up."

"So who are we after?" asked Jack, adjusting his glasses.

"Snivel has all the material for a full briefing,"

Bob told them, "he'll tell you everything you need to know."

Half an hour later Jack and his friends were in the tree house that he and Oscar shared. It was a *magnificent* tree house, basically a converted shed that Oscar's dad had won and had then installed in the massive oak tree that grew at the end of their garden. Oscar's garden backed onto Jack's, making the tree house a great meeting place between their homes. It was used as a base for all their adventures and housed Jack's workshop, where he developed and made many of his brilliant inventions.

Since the arrival of Snivel it had also become the unofficial headquarters for Jack's small group of GUNGE agents.

Ruby, Oscar and Jack settled themselves

down on cushions and waited for Snivel to begin the briefing. The robot dog tapped his nose and a holographic screen appeared in midair, beamed out of his third eye.

On the holographic screen an image appeared. The alien was some kind of giant insect, with thin hairy legs, bulbous eyes and a long thin proboscis.

"Looks like a giant tick," muttered Jack.

"I'd give it a cross myself," said Ruby.

Jack and Oscar stared at her blankly.

"You know, like on your homework. Jack said it looks like a tick, like, when you've got something right and the teacher ticks your paper, and I said it was more like a cross, you know, when the teacher puts a red cross because it's not right and—"

"Yeah," said Oscar, sarcastically. "Good one."

Ruby scowled.

"This insect-like creature is a Burrapong,"

explained Snivel, cutting off their bickering. "And to track it down you're going to need your noses."

Snivel crossed his eyes in concentration and, without warning, produced a terrible raspberry noise.

"Ugh!" exclaimed Oscar as an awful sulphurous odour filled the tree house. "The robot dog farted!"

"That is merely an example of the atmosphere on the Burrapong home planet," explained Snivel. "I thought it would be best to let you experience it for yourselves."

"So you let one off?" said Oscar, with disgust.

Ruby was holding her nose and backing towards the exit. "That is rank!" she said.

The others agreed – the smell in the confined space of the tree house was unbearable. Ruby

and Jack squeezed out through the door, as Oscar jumped through the window.

CRASH! Somehow, Oscar had completely failed to grab hold of any the tree's branches as he fell through them to the ground.

"Ouch," he muttered, as he got to his feet, covered in mud.

CHAPTER THREE

It was half an hour before they could face being inside again. While they waited, Oscar popped home to fetch them some snacks. When he returned he was waving a hand in front of his nose.

"It was pretty bad at home too," he explained. "Dad's on night shifts this week so he's at home watching TV, and I tell you, my dad farts like a trooper."

"Nothing could be as bad as that smell Snivel just made," said Jack.

"Don't bet on it," said Oscar, pulling a face.

The three children returned to the tree house to resume the briefing.

Snivel reactivated his hologram and displayed the Burrapong again.

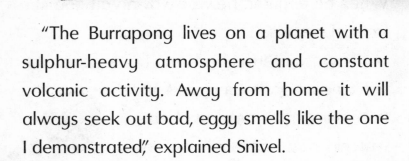

"The Burrapong lives on a planet with a sulphur-heavy atmosphere and constant volcanic activity. Away from home it will always seek out bad, eggy smells like the one I demonstrated," explained Snivel.

"No need to repeat that bit," said Jack quickly.

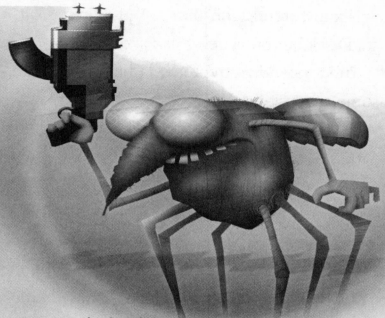

"As with the first alien you caught this one will be in a human disguise. But wherever he is, it'll be smelly."

"Great," muttered Oscar.

Ruby got to her feet and began examining the things on Jack's worktable. "You got any gadgets that will help us with this one, Jack?"

she asked picking up something that looked like a wooden recorder.

"Hey, careful with that – I just finished it," said Jack, jumping up.

Ruby looked at the thing in her hands with some confusion.

"It's a recorder," she said with some disdain. "You can't *invent* a recorder, it's already been done. I've got one for music class. Well, *Mum* thinks it's music class, anyway. Actually it's when I have my taekwondo lessons."

Oscar nodded his head in agreement. "Yeah, they've been around at least three years – we had a recorder group when I was in Year One."

Jack tutted and shook his head sadly. He reached out a hand for his invention. Ruby passed it to him and Jack turned it so that the labels on each of the instrument's holes were visible. Each label had an instruction on it –

'play dead', 'sit', 'beg', 'forward', 'left'...

"It's a special dog whistle," said Jack. "I saw some old shepherd bloke controlling his sheepdog with whistles, and it gave me an idea. With this, any dog becomes like a remote-controlled toy. You can make it go backwards, forwards, left, right, up—"

"Yes," interrupted Oscar. "We get the idea."

"But don't you have to train the dog first, to respond to the different sounds?" asked Ruby.

"That's just it. The shepherd bloke does and it takes years but this works directly on the dog's brainwaves and makes it do what you want."

Oscar was frowning. "Why are you always making inventions for dogs?" he asked. "You haven't got one!"

"Oy!" said Snivel, blinking his three eyes rapidly.

"You don't count," replied Oscar. "You've got three eyes and sometimes you leak oil."

Jack slipped the recorder into his pocket. "Anyway, this isn't going to help us find the fart-loving alien, is it?"

"Where do we start then?" asked Oscar.

Jack gave it some thought. "Well, if the alien likes farts, it's going to seek out the worst farters in town."

Oscar grinned. "Then that's got to be my dad. His farts are evil."

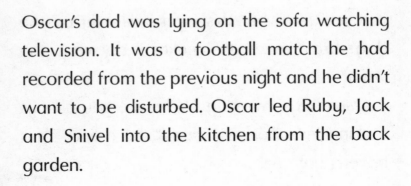

Oscar's dad was lying on the sofa watching television. It was a football match he had recorded from the previous night and he didn't want to be disturbed. Oscar led Ruby, Jack and Snivel into the kitchen from the back garden.

"Whatever you do, don't tell him the score," Oscar whispered.

"No danger of that," said Jack. "I don't know the score." Football wasn't really his thing. Actually, anything involving physical activity wasn't really his thing.

Ruby rolled her eyes and sighed. "England won three–nil," she told him. "Rooney, Walcott and Heskey."

Oscar hushed her. "Ssh – keep it quiet. He likes to watch it without knowing what happens."

Suddenly, there was a loud retort from the direction of the lounge. BRAAAAP!

"Was that…?" began Ruby.

Oscar nodded. "I told you he could fart for England."

The three of them waited but no alien appeared. "Give it time," said Oscar, "by half-time it'll be like a swamp in there."

Jack was looking around at the layout of the house, searching for access points a fart-loving alien could use to get in.

"We need to be closer to the action," he said.

Ruby sniffed and caught a whiff of the smell coming from the lounge. "I think that's a job for you," she said, pulling a face.

Jack nodded. "Oscar, create a diversion. Snivel and I will sneak behind the sofa and wait for the alien to turn up."

Oscar held his breath as he walked into the room and stood close to the TV.

"Hi, Dad," he said, "how's it going?" His voice went a bit squeaky towards the end, as he ran out of air. He took a breath and grimaced.

"Still nil-nil," said Oscar's dad, without enthusiasm. "We're playing like a bunch of schoolboys. No offence."

"None taken," replied Oscar. "Can I get you anything?"

Oscar's dad just looked at him. "Have you been abducted by aliens and replaced with a robot?" he asked, astonished at Oscar's offer.

"I was just asking. No need to be like that," said Oscar. Over his dad's head he could see a small hand sticking up behind the sofa giving him a thumbs up sign. "I'll be in the kitchen if you need anything..." He left the room.

Behind the sofa, Jack and Snivel settled down to wait. It didn't take long. Oscar's Dad shuffled his position and let off a tremendous fart. Jack pinched his nose – the smell was awful. Moments later Oscar's dad repeated his trick and this time it was even worse. Surely any alien interested in farts would want to experience this?

Suddenly the door pushed open and a cat sauntered into the room, purring as it jumped up onto Oscar's dad's lap.

It had to be the alien!

"Go!" ordered Jack, leaping out from behind the sofa. He made a grab for the cat but the feline had spotted Snivel and leapt up, claws extended.

"Ow!" Jack's arms were scratched badly by the cat's claws as it squirmed out of his grasp and shot off, closely followed by Snivel. Disturbed by the commotion, Oscar's dad was immediately on his feet.

"What the—" He paused, as he processed

who was standing in front of him. "Jack? What are you doing there?"

Jack got to his feet and thought rapidly.

"Sorry," he said quickly, "I just wanted to see the goal."

"What goal? There hasn't been a goal."

"The Rooney goal?" suggested Jack, hopefully. "Or the Heskey one. Or maybe the Walcott one?"

"Three goals?! There's not been one yet! Thanks a lot, Jack. I didn't want any spoilers."

Hearing the shouting, Oscar appeared at the door.

"He's talking about a game we played on the computer, Dad, don't worry about it. Come on, Jack..."

Jack allowed himself to be pulled out of the lounge and back to the kitchen where Ruby bathed his scratches with warm water.

A few moments later Snivel reappeared. Like his master he too was covered in scratches.

"The cat," he announced with a sigh, "is just a cat! She's called Princess."

Ruby looked at Oscar, raising one eyebrow.

"My mum chose the name, all right?" said Oscar.

Jack looked at his friends. "We need to give this some more thought."

CHAPTER FOUR

Back in the tree house the three friends put their heads together and tried some serious thinking. Where in town might the alien have hidden himself? Where would he get an unlimited supply of malodorous gases?

Oscar couldn't get away from the idea that the prime source for such noxious fumes was farts and proceeded to make a long list of relatives who, he claimed, could fart for Britain.

"Are your family completely disgusting or what?" muttered Ruby.

"Well, I'm all right, aren't I?" asked Oscar.

"Suppose so," said Ruby.

Then Oscar completely ruined the moment by blowing off in a noisy and smelly fashion.

Oscar and Snivel found this very amusing but Ruby and Jack were more focused on the problem at hand.

"Let's make a list," suggested Jack, "of all the

places that might have the sulphur smell this Burrapong prefers."

Ruby nodded and fetched a large piece of paper and a felt-tip pen. "Right," she said, sitting back down. "Fire away."

The boys looked at each other, smiling. Oscar leaned to the side, as if to let out a fart. "With your *ideas*," she explained. "Keep your bottoms under control!"

They began to brainstorm some possibilities: the sewage plant on the edge of town, the municipal dump, the hot springs, the pig farm... Finally they had a short list of the five most likely locations.

For the rest of the day they worked their way, slowly and methodically, down the list.

At the fart-machine factory they were chased away by a security guard for trespassing. At the dump they found piles of rubbish but no sign of any alien. The hot springs were closed – apparently the recent drought had affected the ancient site and limited the supply of sulphurous bubbling water. The pig farm was smelly but full of next week's sausages, not alien invaders. Finally, the three heroes reached the sewage works. Surely this was

a place that would be irresistible to the Burrapong?

As they approached the works they could see large buildings, surrounded with pipes of various sizes. But there was a complete lack of any kind of bad smell.

"Has this place gone out of business?" Jack

wondered as they walked up to the main gate. A thin woman in a smart suit appeared and seemed to be delighted to see them.

"Ah, visitors!" she announced. "Come this way. You're the first today…"

"I'm not surprised," muttered Ruby to Jack. "Who comes to a sewage plant for fun?"

The woman, who introduced herself as Kathie, had

other ideas. She gave them a full tour, explaining in mind-numbing detail all the very clever (if rather boring) scientific advances that the company had recently developed to minimise odour.

"We're the sweetest-smelling sewage plant in the country," Kathie told them with pride.

"Nothing for our alien here then," whispered Jack, despondently.

"What was that?" asked Kathie eagerly.

"I was just saying how amazing it all is," he lied.

Kathie beamed. Jack, Ruby and Oscar fixed similar grins to their faces and endured the rest of the tour.

At the end of the day Jack was sitting with Snivel on the sofa watching TV with his mum. She was a nurse at the hospital and worked lots of night shifts, so it was a rare treat to have an evening with her in front of the television. Jack tried to maintain the illusion of being interested in the programmes his mum chose to watch, but it was difficult to concentrate. All he could think about was the Burrapong. The alien was out there somewhere – somewhere close. But where? It had to be somewhere that would replicate the smelly, sulphur-rich atmosphere of its home planet… but, after their exhaustive search had failed to locate it, where in town could it possibly be? There had to be an answer, but for the life of him Jack couldn't think of one.

On the television screen some meerkats were playing around in a zoo enclosure, popping out of various holes and looking like they were playing Hide and Seek. The programme was *Zoo Watch Live Update*, one of

Mum's favourites. It came on every summer and featured a different zoo every year.

"Oh, I like meerkats," Mum said. "Remember when we went to see them when you were two?"

Jack just shot his Mum a look – how could he remember something that happened when he was two?

"Look, that's where you were standing when you dropped your ice-cream cone into the enclosure."

Jack sat up. "You mean that's our local zoo?"

Now it was his mum's turn to shoot a sharp look at him. "Yes, Jack, I told you last week. This year *Zoo Watch Live Update* is coming from our very own zoo here in town. Isn't that exciting?"

Jack had to agree that it was exciting, but not as exciting as the thought he'd just had.

The last time he'd gone to the zoo the one thing he remembered about it was that it had been absolutely stinking. The gorilla cages were smelly, the capybara enclosure was a nightmare but the worst, most offensive stench of all came from…

"Elephants," said the bubbly blonde host of *Zoo Watch Live Update*, a pretty girl called, for no good reason that Jack could see, Zana. "Surely everyone's favourite zoo creatures. I know they're mine," said Zana as the camera pulled back to see that she was walking through the elephant enclosure. Behind her a large elephant was quietly having a wee, forming a steaming stream that was moving unstoppably towards Zana's brand-new-looking safari boots.

Zana had only recently started working on grown-up TV, having spent years on kids' shows, working with an assortment of naff puppets. Until recently she had been the host of *Animal Ark*, and Jack remembered that she had an unfortunate habit of getting poo-ed on, bitten, scratched and generally humiliated by every different kind of creature that they featured. The episode where the grass snake disappeared down her blouse while she was interviewing the snake handler was a classic that was still spoken about in playgrounds months after its initial broadcast. Jack sat up, hoping that Zana's luck hadn't changed recently.

"This here is Charlie," said Zana, now standing next to another elephant. She stroked its trunk nervously and smiled at the camera without conviction. "Isn't he just the most beautiful creature?" she asked rhetorically. With brilliant comic timing Charlie the elephant punctuated her sentence with an enormous fart, making a noise so loud that the camera shook. "And so gentle," continued Zana bravely, but had to stop as the smell hit her nostrils and she began to turn green.

"That's rank!" came a voice from behind the camera, as the stench reached the cameraman.

Without warning the programme cut away to some more footage of the meerkats.

"Oh, that's a shame," said Jack's mum. "I like the elephants."

But Jack was no longer on the sofa. He was running up the stairs to phone his friends. Elephants might well be his mum's favourites and Zana's too but there was someone else he was sure would love the foul-smelling fart-producing pachyderms – the alien Burrapong!

The next day couldn't come quickly enough. As soon as they were able, the three friends assembled at the tree house. Snivel had been able to record the previous night's edition of *Zoo Watch Live Update*, and now he played back the clip using his holographic projector.

"What do you think?" asked Jack.

"Not as funny as that one where the snake escaped," said Oscar, giggling at the memory.

"It's not her fault she's too stupid to walk and

talk at the same time," said Ruby.

"I'm not talking about Zana – I'm talking about that farting elephant at our local zoo!" pointed out Jack.

"Oh," said Oscar.

"Right," said Ruby.

Both looked a bit embarrassed.

"Well?" asked Jack.

Ruby and Oscar looked at each other and shrugged. After the previous day's failures they seemed to have lost their enthusiasm.

"Come on," said Jack, "we can't give up. The Squillibloat was real, wasn't it? So is the Burrapong and we've got to find it."

Jack explained his theory to his friends. He was sure the Burrapong had infiltrated the zoo and slimed the elephant keeper. Now wearing a disguise to make him look like the trapped keeper, he was probably hoovering up those big elephant farts like there was no tomorrow.

"And remember," Jack concluded sternly, "if the aliens get together and use the Blower there really will be no tomorrow."

Ruby and Oscar agreed that the zoo was at least worth a look, but there was just one problem.

"I'm skint," said Oscar.

"Me too," added Ruby. "All my pocket money is going on climbing lessons right now. How about you?"

Jack had to confess that he too was lacking in funds.

"Can't we claim expenses from GUNGE?" he asked Snivel.

Snivel shook his head. "Sorry."

Jack looked back at his friends. "So how do we get into the zoo with no money between us?"

Ruby and Oscar looked blank.

"Maybe we should phone *Zoo Watch Live Update* and cadge a visit with them," joked Oscar.

Jack clicked his fingers. "That's brilliant," he exclaimed, as if Oscar had made a serious suggestion

Oscar grinned. "Yeah, I am, aren't I?" Then the grin faded to be replaced with a confused frown. "Er... Why?"

CHAPTER FIVE

Jack, Ruby, Oscar and Snivel walked across town to the zoo. In the car park, just as Jack had predicted back in the tree house, they found a couple of large vans marked with the logo of the TV Channel who made *Zoo Watch Live Update*. Parked nearby was a modest trailer home.

"That'll be Zana's," said Jack confidently. He strolled across to the trailer home and knocked on the door. "Play along," he whispered to his friends. The door opened and Zana appeared. She seemed a little less bouncy and bubbly in the flesh but as soon as she saw that her visitors were children she switched on her TV personality.

"Hi there," she said, giving them a smile that showed off all the fancy dental work her father had spent so much money on. "What can I do for you guys?"

Jack started to tell her what big fans they were of her and her new show.

"We still miss *Animal Ark*, though," said Oscar, forgetting Jack's instructions to leave the talking to him. Ruby jabbed him in the chest with her elbow.

"But *Zoo Watch Live Update* is our favourite," Jack continued. "Although this series is making me really sad."

Zana managed to compose her features into an expression of concern. "Sad? Why is it making you sad, honey?" she asked.

Jack explained that it was so hard seeing their local zoo on the TV when they couldn't afford to go for real. Jack made a big thing about having a single mum and not a lot of money. Both of which were basically true, actually.

Zana was touched by his story. Well, at least that's what she told Jack. In reality she was thinking that the children would make a great item for the show. Her producer was always yelling at her to make more of a creative contribution. Well, now she had one. Some local kids, unable to visit the zoo because of personal circumstances, would get a chance to see all their favourite animals courtesy of *Zoo Watch Live Update*. Brilliant TV. She'd probably get her own chat show out of this.

Thirty minutes later she had pitched the idea to her producer and been given the green light. There'd been a bit of a hiccup with the zoo authorities about Jack's dog, but Jack had put on a great performance of a child about to burst into tears and the men in suits had decided to allow Snivel to stay with Jack – as long as he remained on a lead.

"Where did you learn to act like that?" asked Ruby as they were allowed through the zoo turnstiles. "That was brilliant bottom-lip quivering."

"Watching those stupid soaps my mum likes," explained Jack, with a grin.

Zana took them through to the gorilla house where the TV crew were setting up to do some recording. "Although it's called *Live Update* we do pre-record a lot of segments," Zana explained. She told them that she needed to do some pick-ups for some material they shot yesterday and that they would be ready to start shooting with the three kids in a couple of hours' time.

"Why don't we have a look around?" suggested Jack helpfully. "Maybe we can spot some of our favourite animals that we can talk about when you interview us."

"Brilliant idea," said Zana. "Meet me back here."

Jack, Ruby, Oscar and Snivel hurried off, grateful to get away from the overbearing TV host.

"What's your mum going to say when she sees you on TV tonight?" wondered Oscar.

"Never mind about that," said Jack. "We need to find the alien first, remember? Now – where's the elephant house?"

"I know a short cut," said Oscar. "Follow me."

"Are you sure about this?"

Jack watched nervously as Oscar fiddled with the lock on a metal door.

"Yeah, of course I am," said Oscar. "There's a whole maze of backstage alleys that the keepers use to get around the different enclosures

and if we go through here we'll get to them."
Oscar's lock-picking worked and the door
sprung open. "Come on..."

Jack, Ruby and Snivel followed Oscar
through the door, which swung shut behind
them. They found themselves in the shade of
some trees.

"Where's the path?" wondered Ruby.

"Must be over this way," said Oscar, moving
towards some light.

"I can see a path," said Jack, pointing. "Over
there."

Ruby looked in the direction Jack was
pointing.

"But that's the other side of the fence..."

Suddenly they heard a chilling howl. Oscar
stopped dead in his tracks and the others
careered into him.

"What's that?" he whispered.

The howl came again, and was joined by

another. And they both sounded very close.

"I've got a bad feeling about this…" muttered Jack.

Something was moving in the bushes near to them.

"I've got a plan," said Oscar, smartly.

"I'm all ears," replied Jack.

"RUN!" suggested Oscar.

They ran. And the creatures whose enclosure they had stumbled into ran too. Yelping, howling and barking at the intruders, a half-dozen animals chased the three children and the robot dog.

"Wolves!" screamed Oscar, as one snapped at his heels and nearly took a bite out of his bum. Jack felt his heart pounding in his chest as he ran away from the furious predators. But then Snivel turned around and activated his third eye, which flashed yellow and emitted a blast of high-pitched sound.

The wolves stopped, whining. They lowered their heads as if in pain.

"Just in time," gasped Ruby. Jack saw that they had reached a dead end – in front of them was a rugged cliff face that formed the end of the wolf enclosure. Behind them the six wolves spread out in a semi-circle around them, waiting. Jack could tell that whatever Snivel had done to them was  wearing off. They didn't look pained now. Just angry.

"My sonic blast worked once," said Snivel. "But without some more snot I won't have enough power for another dose." Snivel had

been constructed out of bits of alien technology, so he ran on alien fuel: snot!

"Well, don't look at me," said Ruby. "*I* blow my nose."

Oscar used his finger to rummage experimentally in his nostrils. "Sorry," he said.

"We have to get out of here," Jack said.

Ruby was shrugging out of her backpack and unzipping it. She quickly pulled out her special climbing shoes and put them on.

73

"Only one way to go," she told them, "and that's up."

Jack and Oscar craned their necks and looked up at the cliff face. It was very steep.

"Cool!" said Oscar, who was never happier than when facing an insanely dangerous challenge.

"No way!" said Jack, who preferred to live a pain-free existence.

But Ruby was already on the wall. Finding foot and hand holds with apparent ease she was quickly halfway up the cliff.

"I've got rope," she called down to them. "When I'm at the top I'll throw it down and you can use it to help you climb."

Moments later she disappeared from sight. Jack and Oscar waited nervously. Behind them the wolves stirred and shuffled a little bit closer.

"What's keeping her?" wondered Oscar.

The end of a thin rope dropped at their feet from above.

Jack passed it to Oscar. "You go first. Then you and Ruby can haul me up."

Oscar shook his head. "I can't leave you down here alone."

One of the wolves chose that moment to growl in a low threatening manner.

"Then again," continued Oscar, "maybe you're right." He grabbed the rope and quickly used it to help him climb to the top.

"Just you and me then," said Jack to Snivel.

"Don't worry about me," said Snivel, and promptly ran up the wall as if it was horizontal rather than vertical.

"Oh, great," muttered Jack to himself.

Behind him the wolves stirred again. Suddenly there was a crashing sound from above.

"Oscar, you clumsy oaf!" shouted Ruby, furiously.

Something was falling towards him. Jack took a step back and the rope fell at his feet – all of it! Now how was he going to get up the wall?

Jack looked at the cliff face again. He could see the first hand- and footholds that Ruby had used but after that it wasn't so clear. This was SO not his area of expertise. Jack just couldn't do it. He was an inventor not an action hero. There must be something he had that might help. He checked his pockets quickly and came across... his new improved dog whistle. Wolves were a kind of dogs, weren't they? Maybe...

Jack put the instrument to his lips, covered the hole marked 'Roll over' with a finger and blew.

Nothing happened. The sound was too high-pitched to be heard by human ears anyway but he had hoped to see some effect on the wolves. Unfortunately they were still slowly closing in on him. He tried again.

Same result. But this time there was something else. A sort of "ooh" sound like the noise a crowd makes when watching fireworks or a man juggling. It was coming from somewhere far away on the other side of the wall.

Jack tried another command. This time he

went for 'Sit'. Again the dog whistle had no effect on the wolves but the crowd – wherever they were – made another 'ooh' sound and followed it with a smattering of applause. Something was impressing *them* at least. If only something would impress the wolves.

Suddenly a new rope dropped down beside him.

"Grab hold!" shouted Oscar.

Jack wrapped the rope around his waist and held on. Ruby and Oscar pulled and he began to rise into the air. And not a moment too soon – the wolves were almost upon him. They snapped angrily at his heels as he disappeared into the air. A few moments later his friends hauled him over the lip of the cliff and he was able to clamber over a low wall back into the human-populated area of the zoo.

"The elephants are just over here," said Ruby. She began to lead the way. As the trio walked they passed a young girl in a pushchair being wheeled along by her mother.

"Mummy, how did they make the elephant roll over and sit like that?" asked the little girl.

Jack looked at the dog whistle. Was it possible? Could his invention have worked on the elephant?

cHApTER sIx

The elephant enclosure was one of the largest in the zoo. It was fronted by a large courtyard in which the elephants could be seen playing in a massive mud bath. At the back of the courtyard were several connected buildings which the elephants could sleep in. In front of the main arena was a deep moat-like trough separating the elephants from their visitors.

Jack thought initially that this was a safety feature but then one of the elephants farted and Jack realised that the distance between humans and elephants was essential. The smell was absolutely disgusting. Much worse than anything they'd encountered while searching for the Burrapong so far.

"That's even worse than my dad's farts," said Oscar with feeling – and he was right.

But while Jack and his friends were forced to hold their noses at the rancid stench there was one person who seemed to be actually *enjoying* it. There was a single zoo keeper on duty in the elephant house; a hairy, bearded and slightly overweight man in his twenties, squeezed into the regulation zoo employee green overalls. There was something just a little bit wrong about the man. Jack wasn't sure what it was but there was *definitely* something. Maybe the hair was just a little bit lifeless, the skin just a touch too rubbery.

Or maybe it was the way the keeper was bending into the path of the elephant's fart and taking an enormous deep breath.

"That's him, isn't it?" said Ruby excitedly. Although she had been a major part of catching their first alien she hadn't been with them when they'd first identified it. This was all new to her.

Jack nodded. He felt a little more at home with this alien-spotting now. As they watched, another elephant let rip and the keeper/alien ran across the enclosure to suck up the odour into his nostrils.

"That's just disgusting," commented Ruby, pulling a face.

"Well, he won't be around long now," said Oscar confidently. "We'll just send Snivel in, Jack can shout the magic words and *wham*! Snivel will turn into his trap form and suck the sucker in. Job done."

Ruby shook her head. "Don't you ever pay attention?" she asked him.

Oscar shrugged. "What? What did I forget?"

"The communications thing, the whatch-macallit in four bits... we have to find the Burrapong's bit of the wotsit," Ruby reminded him.

"The whatchmacallit wotsit?" repeated

Oscar, not following at all.

"The Blower!" explained Jack patiently. "We have get hold of this guy's segment of the Blower before we can trap him."

The three of them took a closer look at the keeper and the enclosure.

"Well, he's not wearing it round his neck like the last one," said Jack.

"So where is it?" asked Ruby. "More to the point – what does it look like?"

Snivel spoke up. "It could look like anything," he explained.

"Well, that's a lot of help," muttered Ruby, not at all impressed.

"Sorry," said Snivel, "but that's the best I can do."

Oscar scratched his head. "The last one was disguised as a necklace, wasn't it?"

Jack nodded. "It sort of glowed," he recalled.

Oscar nodded. "Yeah, it did, didn't it? A bit like that elephant's earring."

Ruby nudged Oscar with her elbow. "Stop mucking about – who ever heard of an elephant with an earring?"

Oscar pulled a face. "I dunno but that one over there has got one – look."

They looked at the elephant Oscar was pointing at. It was the largest elephant in the enclosure – a massive giant that must have been nearly three metres tall. It also seemed to be the moodiest. It was banging its head against a tyre hanging from a tree branch and making angry grunting noises. In one of its massive flapping ears it had a sort of stud earring – an earring that glowed with a strangely familiar blue light.

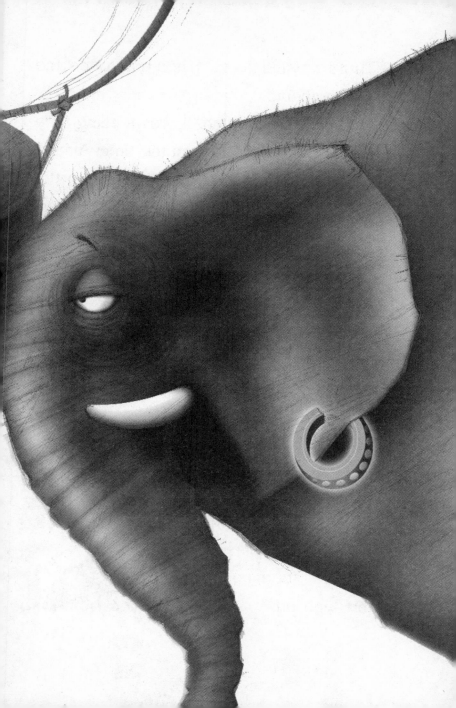

"That's it," said Jack. "That has to be the blower segment."

He checked his watch. It was feeding time at the penguins in thirty minutes' time. Almost everyone at the zoo would converge on the penguins' enclosure for that, making it the best time to make their attempt at the elephant. He explained his thinking to the others.

"But what about trapping the alien?" asked Snivel after Jack had explained his plan.

"We'll deal with that part when we get to it," said Jack, "but the first thing is to secure that part of the Blower."

Oscar sneaked into the keeper's office and 'borrowed' a bag labelled 'Elephants' Treats'. He returned to the others and gave them a thumbs-up sign.

Jack smiled. Everything was coming together.

Jack was so excited he didn't notice Ruby powdering her hands. She had her own plan – and it was far more exciting and dangerous than his.

"I wonder why the blower part is on the elephant," said Jack as they returned to the front of the enclosure. "You'd think the alien would keep it somewhere safe."

"It's on top of the elephant creature," said Snivel. "How much safer can you get?"

Ruby grinned. "A lot, at least when I'm around."

"What are you talking about?" asked Jack.

"Your plan is too complicated," she told him. "I'll just climb up him and take the wotsit."

"Blower part," Jack corrected her automatically.

"Whatever."

Oscar looked at the elephant and then back at Ruby. "It's not like a wall, you know. It moves. What if it chucks you off?"

Ruby shrugged. "It's not going to chuck me off. I went on a bucking bronco ride at the fair last year and they had to pay me to get off I was on it for so long."

Oscar looked at Ruby and pulled a face. He was half annoyed and half impressed. Jack had to stop himself from laughing. Sometimes Ruby seemed to out-Oscar Oscar.

"Look I can easily climb the elephant and get the..." Ruby paused and then, after making a real effort of memory, said, "Blower bit."

Oscar and Jack still looked doubtful.

"You wouldn't have got hold of the first bit without my surfing skills," she reminded them.

Oscar and Jack sighed. Ruby was the kind of girl you just couldn't argue with.

"OK," said Jack, "You're on."

CHAPTER SEVEN

The first part of the plan was the easiest. Getting into the actual elephant enclosure wasn't too difficult. Oscar's lock-picking soon had them through a gate which gave them access. As Jack had predicted, the crowds had hurried off to see feeding time with the penguins and, with no one around to watch them, most of the elephants had trudged inside.

The giant elephant that was of most interest to Jack and his friends was standing in one of the hay-filled bays, relaxing – exactly how they wanted him. Jack smiled at Ruby.

Oscar opened the bag of elephant treats and approached the giant pachyderm. "Here you are, Jumbo, just for you…" he said, holding the bag out. The elephant reached out with his trunk and took something from the bag. It was an apple. The elephant bent his trunk back and popped the apple into his mouth.

"Plenty more where that came from," offered Oscar, stroking the elephant's trunk with his other hand.

"Are you sure you're up for this?" Jack asked Ruby.

"Absolutely," she said with a grin. While Oscar kept the elephant occupied she quickly used her climbing skills to shimmy up the trunk and onto his head. From there she got herself into position on the elephant's shoulders. Now she could begin to reach down towards the ear where the mysterious earring was glowing.

Suddenly there was a horrified cry.

"Oy!" It was the elephant keeper, and he was standing in the doorway. With the terrifying sound of a plum splitting, but amplified about a thousand times, the alien abandoned its disguise, shedding and shredding his 'human' skin to reveal his true form. It was even worse in the flesh than it had been in Snivel's hologram projection. It was like looking at a giant insect, a bit like a cross between a house fly and a mosquito. Despite losing its human disguise it was still capable of speech.

"Get away from there, human half-grown!" it screeched in a high-pitched tone. "Or I will suck your friend dry."

Without warning it pounced on Oscar, pulling him to the ground.

Petrified, Oscar broke wind. The alien roared with delight. "Let the harvest begin!" it cried and thrust its head directly towards poor Oscar's bum.

While Jack looked on in horror, the alien took a deep breath and began to expand. Before his very eyes the Burrapong was getting bigger.

Oscar's cheeks were sucked in and his eyes bulged. A horrible squeal came from his mouth.

"It's vacuuming up his farts!" said Snivel. "All of them. We have to stop him before he pulls Oscar inside out!"

Jack looked around in panic. There had to be something round here that might help. What would they do if one of the elephants went on a rampage? Then he saw it, a tranquiliser gun set in a glass case marked 'Break in case of emergency'.

Jack was fairly certain that imminent danger of a child being sucked inside out by an alien was not the kind of emergency anyone at the zoo had in mind when they had installed the gun – but it had to count.

Without a second thought, Jack broke the glass and grabbed the gun. He pointed it

at the alien, which was now twice the size it had been originally and bloated like a balloon. Jack squeezed the trigger and was delighted when the alien popped and deflated so quickly it flew off across the room like a burst balloon.

Unfortunately the sound of bursting balloons was the one thing in the world that scared the giant elephant. He reared up, just as Ruby was extracting the earring from his ear. Somehow she just managed to hang on as the elephant trumpeted in fear and reared up again.

Jack reviewed the situation as quickly as he could. Oscar was still lying on the floor recovering from his ordeal. Slowly, his body filled out again as air from his lungs replaced his farts. Ruby was barely hanging on to the frightened giant elephant and the alien... oh no, and the alien was getting to its feet.

Deflated it might be but it clearly wasn't defeated. Jack dropped the gun – he couldn't use that again, not now the alien was all out of gas. He had to find another weapon. Or a tool or something. If only he could invent something that would get him out of a scrape like this. And then it hit him – maybe he *had*. He pulled out his super-improved dog whistle. Covering the hole marked 'Stay' he blew into it. Immediately the elephant responded and stood still.

"Come on down," said Jack.

Ruby didn't have to be told twice. Quickly she slid down the trunk and jumped clear. Oscar was struggling to his feet. "Got it!" shouted Ruby, holding up the glowing earring.

"Look out, Jack," cried Oscar, "he's still coming!"

Jack looked round and saw that the Burrapong was edging ever closer, dragging one of his many legs, presumably where he had been injured. Jack looked at the dog whistle in his hands. Of course! Quickly he put it to his lips again and blew 'Left'. The elephant moved to his left, closer to the alien. *Brilliant*, thought Jack, *I've got the world's first remote-control elephant.*

He blew the command for forward, then right, back... Quickly he manoeuvred the elephant into position. One more step and then... SIT!

SPLAT!

The elephant sat down exactly where Jack wanted it to, directly over the disgusting alien.

The Burrapong disappeared into its giant bum.

"Snivel," Jack called. "Get into position."

Snivel ran around to the back to the elephant and stood ready. He realised exactly what Jack was trying to do.

Jack raised the dog whistle to his mouth again and blew it, covering the hole marked 'Stand'.

Instantly the elephant stood up again, revealing the hairy back legs of the alien sticking out of its bum. The alien legs wiggled and jiggled as the Burrapong tried to work itself free.

Snivel took a step forward and placed himself directly under the elephant's bottom.

"Activate Snivel Trap!" shouted Jack.

The alien technology that was hidden inside the heart of the robot dog sprang into action, transforming the hairy four-legged (and three-eyed) creature into a snap-lidded metallic box.

With a final effort the Burrapong managed to wriggle almost free from the elephant's bum.

Jack blew 'Sit' again and the elephant sat back down again. As soon as the alien's feet touched the Snivel Trap it activated. There was an enormous sucking sound and the elephant briefly went cross-eyed. Oscar offered it another snack and it stepped forward, revealing the Snivel Trap all shut up.

They'd done it. Again!

"Oh my goodness!" a shrill voice broke the

silence that had descended. Jack span round. Now what?

It was Zana from *Zoo Watch Live Update*. Unseen by the children she must have come into the elephant house sometime during the chaos – and from the stunned expression on her face she had seen everything!

"That was incredible – what was that?" she asked, her face as white as a sheet.

"Nothing," said Jack, unable to come up with a convincing lie on the spot. "It was absolutely nothing."

Picking up the Snivel Trap he headed for the door. Ruby and Oscar followed him.

"But… but…" stammered Zana demonstrating something Jack's mother often said, namely that TV presenters couldn't string a sentence together without a script to read out.

"What about the programme?" she managed to get out as the trio filed out past her.

"Sorry," said Jack. "My dog ran off, we need to go and find him."

"But you're going to be on TV, I'm going to interview you about your favourite zoo animal. Is it elephants?"

"I've gone off elephants," said Ruby with feeling.

Leaving the poor TV presenter with her mouth hanging open in shock, the children ran off. They needed to get the alien safely to Bob and get him to find the real zoo keeper as quickly as possible.

As they left the zoo Ruby brought up the subject of Zana.

"What are we going to do about her off the telly?" she asked.

"Don't worry about it," said Jack, crossing his fingers for luck. "Who's going to believe an airhead like that?"

Back in the elephant house Zana was getting over her shock. She wasn't sure exactly what it was that she had seen but she was sure she'd seen something. Something pretty unusual. Something pretty newsworthy.

Jack was wrong about Zana. She actually

wasn't entirely an airhead. In fact once upon a time she'd been considered quite bright by her teachers at journalism college. But somewhere along the line she'd stopped using her intelligence. From getting a break on her local radio station, to making her television debut as a children's TV channel link person, every step in her career seemed to require her to think less and less. Nevertheless, somewhere deep inside her there remained the seed of a journalist. And that long forgotten seed had finally been woken.

Zana realised that somehow she had stumbled upon a story bigger than anything she had ever encountered. Bigger than anything any of her fellow journalism students had dreamed of back at college. And she was determined to make the most of it.

Zana smiled. Today was going to be the start of something big.

PARP! Zara's nose wrinkled in disgust. The elephant had trumped again!

CHAPTER EIGHT

Ruby, Oscar and Jack hurried across town back to the postbox where Bob was now based. When they arrived with the news that they had succeeded with their second mission, Bob was over the moon. Well, he *sounded* over the moon, but once again he remained hidden from sight.

"Why don't you come out to collect him?" said Ruby as Jack placed the Snivel Trap on the ground in front of the postbox.

"No need for that. Not when you have all this technology at your disposal," said Bob proudly. A familiar bright blue light emerged from the slit of the postbox and covered the Snivel Trap. The light did something strange, something akin to a heat haze on a summer's day, the blueness did a sort of wibble, and then the light flashed with an intense brightness that made the children shield their eyes. When they opened them again the Snivel Trap had disappeared and Snivel was sitting there in his dog form again.

"And now the Blower part?" asked the voice of Bob.

Ruby produced the alien earring from her pocket. Up close they could see that it was a kind of printed circuit shaped like an earring.

"Excellent," said Bob as the

earring floated out of Ruby's hand and through the letter slit in the postbox. A moment later there was a faint *clang*.

Oscar sighed. "Is that it? Shouldn't we celebrate with a slap-up pizza or something?"

"Don't worry, Oscar, you'll get your reward for all your hard work… when the rest of the aliens have been captured. You've only done half the work so far."

When Jack got home he found his mum ironing in the living room. She looked a bit fed up. "What's wrong, Mum?'

She shrugged. "I don't know what's going on. *Zoo Watch Live Update*'s been cancelled without warning. They put on some old sitcom instead tonight, one I've seen about a thousand times before."

"So what happened at the zoo?" asked Jack, casting a nervous glance in the direction of Snivel.

"I don't know. There was some kind of incident. A zoo keeper got attacked but he's OK now. But they've decided to finish this series at a different zoo. It's all very mysterious."

"Never mind, Mum," said Jack. "I'm sure it's nothing serious."

Mum went back to her ironing. "And what about you

then? How's my little hero been today? Done anything exciting you can tell your old mum about?"

Jack cast his mind back over the last couple of hours. Sneaking into the zoo, being chased by wolves, playing with a remote-control elephant and catching a dangerous fart-eating alien…

"No," he answered his mum eventually, "nothing exciting at all!"

On the other side of town, in a trans-dimensional impossibility that existed inside a postbox, Bob was checking on his captives. Inside his long dark corridor of glass-walled cells two were now illuminated. In one lay the Squillibloat in a drug-induced sleep, in the next lay the Burrapong, in an artificial fetid atmosphere full of sulphur fumes.

At the end of the corridor was a free-standing shelving unit with four individually lit platforms. On one of the platforms sat the necklace that had been taken from the Squillibloat by the children a few weeks back. Now Bob placed the earring on the second platform. For a brief moment it glowed with a spooky green light, which then faded just as quickly.

Halfway, thought Bob to himself with satisfaction. *Two down and two to go.*

Bob walked back along the corridor, kicking aside the piles of letters and cards which showered down on him regularly in this new location. At least it was better than rubbish. The children had done well. At this rate the mission would soon be accomplished. All four cells would be occupied and the four parts of the Blower would be safely in his hands.

And then… everything would be running to plan and the Earth would be safe…

For now.

Take a sneak peek at book 3 in the Gunk adventure!

Before Jack had a chance to protect himself the alien had wrapped two of its spindly legs around him and pulled him into the air.

"Did you think I could be fooled so easily? I know you've caught two of my... colleagues... but I'm smarter than any blithering Burrapong or stupid Squillibloat!" said the alien proudly.

The Flartibug continued to climb into the air. Jack watched in horror as the ground fell away.

"I am a Flartibug and I am

no fool," hissed the creature. "Now bring me my part of the Blower or I will drop you."

Jack tried to calculate how far up they were now. *Twenty metres? Thirty metres?* Did it really matter? He'd be dead just the same.

This is it, thought Zana. This was the footage that would make her famous. This was going to be big. Bigger than *Newsround.* Bigger than *News at Ten.* This was going to be global.

Just need to make sure I get the best shots. Zana remembered something one of her producers had told her when she had first worked in television. "You can say what you want on television but it only means something to the viewer when they can actually see it. Pictures are the most important bit!"

She wriggled forward so that the remote poked out from under the pile of bin bags, to ensure the signal was clear.

Jack swallowed hard. What was he to do? This far from the ground it was getting very windy, making it even harder to control the helicopter. Snivel was being buffeted around in the gusts of wind.

Frantically Jack worked the remote controls, trying to prevent the chopper flying into the electricity pylon.

The Flartibug looked at the remote control in Jack's hands, then at the helicopter and Snivel suspended beneath it.

"Ah, I see that you are controlling your flying pet with that thing!" it said. Then it leaned in close, grinning at him through its

horrible insect mouth. Its breath stank of rotting filth. "Now," it said, "you will use that device to crash your pet into the ground!"

"What?" exclaimed Jack.

"You heard me, human. Sacrifice your pet and I may choose not to drop you to your certain death."

"What do you mean you *may* choose not to drop me?" demanded Jack.

"Well, it might be fun to watch... But make your dog's crash spectacular enough, and I shall probably be satisfied."

Jack fought his rising panic. *What to do?*

"Getting bored now, " said the alien.

Jack thought desperately. If he crashed the chopper Snivel could be flattened... but if he refused to do as the Flartibug demanded it would be him plummeting towards the grounds and getting spread out across most of the park. *What to do?*

"Time's up," clicked the alien.

With another of its thin hairy limbs the Flartibug snatched the remote control from Jack's hands and tossed it into the air.

"Goodbye, doggy!" it said, laughing.

JONNY MOON

THEY CAME FROM SPACE ... TO GET UP YOUR NOSE!

GUNK
ALIENS
THE VERRUCA BAZOOKA

THE FIRST
GROSSLY FUNNY
GUNK ALIENS ADVENTURE!

Jack loves to invent things – but even he
couldn't make this up. After all, who would
believe that an ordinary nine-year-old boy
would get recruited into a secret agency to
help stop an alien invasion? Well, it's true.
And now Jack and
his friends are all
that stand against
the might of the GUNK
Aliens…

JOIN THE
FIGHT IF YOU
VALUE YOUR
SNOT!

THE THIRD GROSSLY FUNNY GUNK ALIENS ADVENTURE!

The gang face their toughest challenge yet, as they go after a terrifying flying alien. In an epic confrontation, Jack's inventing skills will be tested to the limit, one of his new friends will fall, and all of his courage will be needed when he takes on the worst ordeal of all. Eating a school dinner…

JOIN THE FIGHT IF YOU VALUE YOUR SNOT!

JONNY MOON

THEY CAME FROM SPACE... TO GET UP YOUR NOSE!

GUNK ALIENS
THE SEWERS CRISIS

THE FOURTH
GROSSLY FUNNY
GUNK ALIENS ADVENTURE!

Jack and his friends are nearing the end of their mission, with only one alien left to capture. The best is always saved for last, though, so none of them should be surprised that this particular alien loves only one thing… poo! But at least, once they've made a sickening descent into the sewers, the world should finally be safe. Shouldn't it?

JOIN THE FIGHT IF YOU VALUE YOUR SNOT!